FIREHOU
SAL

SCHOLASTIC INC.
New York Toronto London Auckland Sydney
Mexico City New Delhi Hong Kong Buenos Aires

For Jean Fennacy, Debbie Manning,
and my Petunia's Place family L.D.B.

To Judi with love E.G.

Reading Consultant

LINDA CORNWELL

Learning Resource Consultant
Indiana Department of Education

ISBN 0-516-23795-0

Published by Scholastic Inc.

20 19 18 17 16 15 14 13 9 10/0

Printed in the United States of America 08

First Scholastic printing, October 2001

Listen.

One siren screams.

Lights flash.

Fire Company 1 races away.

Listen.

Two sirens more.

Lights flash.

FIRE COMPANY 2

Fire Company 2 joins the race.

2

Listen.

Three sirens more.

Lights flash.

3
3

Fire Company 3 is on its way.

4
FIRE COMPANY
4

Listen.

Four sirens more.

Lights flash.

Fire Company 4 doesn't want to be last.

4
4

ENT STORE
MAIN
3

Through city streets.

3
3

Over the bay.

How many trucks race from every way?

There's no fire.

5
5

So what's the rush?

Firehouse Sal has had five pups.

Word List (50 Words)

away	flash	more	streets
bay	four	no	the
be	from	on	there's
city	had	one	three
doesn't	has	over	through
every	how	pups	to
fire	is	race	trucks
Fire Company 1	its	races	two
Fire Company 2	joins	rush	want
Fire Company 3	last	screams	way
Fire Company 4	lights	siren	what's
Firehouse Sal	listen	sirens	
five	many	so	

About the Author

Larry Dane Brimner, a native of Florida, grew up in Alaska and California. A teacher for twenty years, he is now the author of more than thirty fiction and nonfiction books for young people.

About the Illustrator

Ethel Gold has illustrated numerous children's books and magazines, and she has created artwork for advertisements and cookbooks. She lives in Southport, Connecticut, with her daughter and two cats.